Dear Parent:
Your child's love of reading starts here!

Every child learns to read in a different way and at his or her own speed. Some go back and forth between reading levels and read favorite books again and again. Others read through each level in order. You can help your young reader improve and become more confident by encouraging his or her own interests and abilities. From books your child reads with you to the first books he or she reads alone, there are I Can Read Books for every stage of reading:

SHARED READING
Basic language, word repetition, and whimsical illustrations, ideal for sharing with your emergent reader

1 BEGINNING READING
Short sentences, familiar words, and simple concepts for children eager to read on their own

2 READING WITH HELP
Engaging stories, longer sentences, and language play for developing readers

3 READING ALONE
Complex plots, challenging vocabulary, and high-interest topics for the independent reader

4 ADVANCED READING
Short paragraphs, chapters, and exciting themes for the perfect bridge to chapter books

I Can Read Books have introduced children to the joy of reading since 1957. Featuring award-winning authors and illustrators and a fabulous cast of beloved characters, I Can Read Books set the standard for beginning readers.

A lifetime of discovery begins with the magical words **"I Can Read!"**

Visit www.icanread.com for information
on enriching your child's reading experience.

I Can Read Book® is a trademark of HarperCollins Publishers.

Huff and Puff Have Too Much Stuff!
Copyright © 2013 by HarperCollins Publishers
All rights reserved. Manufactured in China.
No part of this book may be used or reproduced in any manner whatsoever without written permission except in the case of
brief quotations embodied in critical articles and reviews. For information address HarperCollins Children's Books, a division of
HarperCollins Publishers, 195 Broadway, New York, NY 10007.
www.icanread.com
Library of Congress catalog card number: 2013953806
ISBN 978-0-06-230506-0 (trade bdg.) — ISBN 978-0-06-230505-3 (pbk.)
14 15 16 17 18   SCP   10 9 8 7 6 5 4 3 2 1
❖
First Edition

Huff and Puff Have Too Much Stuff!

by Tish Rabe
pictures by Gill Guile

HARPER
An Imprint of HarperCollinsPublishers

One day Huff said,
"Look at us, Puff!
"We push and pull
a lot of stuff."

6

"That sounds good to me,"
said Puff.

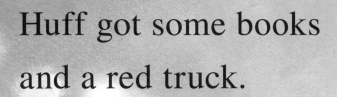

Huff got some books
and a red truck.

"Take us too!"
said some cows and ducks.

Puff got a kite,
a bike, and a boat.

"Take me!" said a goat
in a pretty pink coat.

Huff got rugs, bugs,
cats, hats, and a ball.

Big stuff, small stuff,
they got it ALL!

Huff tried pulling the train
up to the top.

Puff tried pushing the train,
but they had to stop.

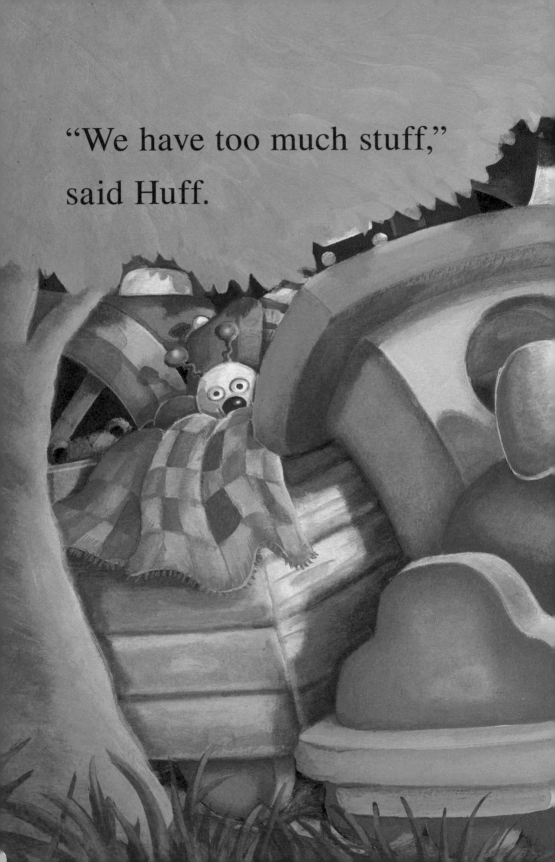

"We have too much stuff,"
said Huff.

"I need stuff,"
said Farmer Fluff.

"I need things to fill my farm.
I need pets to fill my barn."

"You can have our stuff,"
said Huff.

"Welcome to my farm!"
said Farmer Fluff.

"There's lots of room
for pets and stuff."

21

So now there goes
just Huff and Puff.
"We don't need much stuff,"
said Huff.

"We have you and me
and that's . . ."

"... enough!"